NOV 9 1998

THE CRIMSON ELF

Italian Tales of Wisdom

MICHAEL J. CADUTO
ILLUSTRATED BY TOM SARMO

fulcrum kids
Golden, Colorado

My original versions of "The Crimson Elf" and "The Golden Stone" are based on stories found in Elizabeth Mathias and Richard Raspa's *Folktales in America: The Verbal Art of an Immigrant Woman* (1985) and are retold with permission from Wayne State University Press, Detroit, Michigan. In their original form, these stories appear as "The Bloodred Evil Elf" and "The Stone of Gold," pp. 213–217 and pp. 169–174 respectively.

My original version of "Books of Wisdom" is based on a story found in Douglas Adams and Mark Carwardine's *Last Chance to See* (1990) and is retold with permission from Crown Publishers, Inc., New York. In its original form, this story appears as "The Sibylline Books," pp. 215–218.

Text copyright © 1997 by Michael J. Caduto
Illustrations copyright © 1997 by Tom Sarmo
Book design by Alyssa Pumphrey

Library of Congress Cataloging-in-Publication Data

Caduto, Michael J.
   The crimson elf : Italian tales of wisdom / Michael J. Caduto ;
illustrated by Tom Sarmo.
      p. cm.
   Summary: A retelling of six traditional Italian tales featuring
talking animals, wizards, and magical kingdoms.
   ISBN 1-55591-323-7 (hc)
   1. Fairy tales—Italy. [1. Fairy tales. 2. Folklore—Italy.]
I. Sarmo, Tom, ill. II. Title.
PZ8.C117245Cr   1997
398.2'0945—dc21   96-48201
                                                                CIP
                                                                 AC

Printed in the United States of America
0 9 8 7 6 5 4 3 2 1

Fulcrum Publishing
350 Indiana Street, Suite 350
Golden, Colorado 80401-5093
(800) 992-2908 • (303) 277-1623

To my Parents
Raffaele and Esterina

and my Grandparents
Annina and Raffaele Caduto,
Elvira and Salvatore Martone

TABLE OF CONTENTS

Traditional Italian Tales and Storytelling   vii

The Crimson Elf   3

The Golden Stone   11

A Mountain of Contentment   21

Frog Princess   29

The Land of Eternal Life   35

Books of Wisdom   45

Author's Note to Parents, Teachers and Librarians   51

Sources   54

Traditional Italian Tales and Storytelling

A group gathers in the warm, moist aroma of a stable lit by the glow of a lantern. Everyone eats a hearty evening meal, then settles in for a time of sharing with family, friends and neighbors. Children play games while women gossip as they spin hemp and mend clothes. Men talk about the size of the harvest and worry about when the next rains will come.

"Long ago … " says a voice. The storytelling begins. As the tale unfolds amid the rustle of animals, an owl's call drifts from the forest at the edge of the vineyard set in the rolling hills. A look of wonder and unease comes over each face lit by the dim ring of yellow light. Slowly, the darkness deepens. Tales come to life as young eyelids grow heavy with the weight of the hours. Soon, the children will pass from the place of stories to the magical land of dreams.

In days past, this is what traditional storytelling was like in the province of Veneto in northeastern Italy. Villagers often held their community meetings, dances and other social gatherings in stables. It was there, too, between the months of November and March, that elderly men and women passed the old tales on to the children of each new generation.

Traditional Italian stories include the *Märchen*, or fairy tales. These tales of fantasy, such as "Frog Princess," "A Mountain of Contentment" and "The Land of Eternal Life," are filled with magical, supernatural characters and events. Read *The Crimson Elf: Italian Tales of Wisdom* and meet animals that talk, wizards, wise elders, a sinister elf and magical kingdoms where royalty dwell. Among the *Märchen* are many funny tales about figures of authority such as parents, clergy, kings and queens. Fairy tales are the original children's stories of Europe.

Folktales come from the day-to-day lessons of living as human beings who share the world with others. In these stories people choose between being cowardly or brave, foolish or wise, selfish or generous. Here you will discover nuggets of truth such as the secret of contentment and the need for being faithful in love. Learn how faith and courage can help us achieve our goals and how we truly can live forever.

On the following pages are tales about growing up and learning from life's experiences. They help you understand why it is important to obey parents and why it is dangerous to wander off on your own. You are reminded that all people are equal and that true love is more important than wealth or social status. These tales of wonder are filled with the wisdom that will help you live well with other people and the world of nature. Although many things have changed through the ages, there remains a seed of good in every human being. Listen well to these stories and let their wisdom grow the goodness in your own heart.

THE CRIMSON ELF

"Hold my hand," said the elf.

THE CRIMSON ELF

Donatella's village sat in a lush valley on the banks of a beautiful river. She was a young girl who lived with her mother in a modest cottage. Donatella's father had died when the girl was very young. Most of the time, she was well behaved and listened to everything her mother said. But Donatella was curious and insisted that she be allowed to travel with her mother to the marketplace in the neighboring village.

"Donatella," her mother said, "you cannot come with me to the marketplace because the road is a dangerous place for little girls and boys. A mean, ugly ogre lives on the road to the nearby town. It catches children and makes them do terrible things. If that were not enough, there is an evil elf who will offer you many wonderful things to lure you into his trap."

"But mother, you will be there to protect me. Please let me go. Please."

"No, I would not be able to keep a close enough watch as we pass through the dark woods."

The next day, Donatella's mother left to barter some of the cloth she had woven for some food and supplies in the neighboring village. "Donatella, I want you to stay home and take care of the house while I am away. Stay inside and, no matter who knocks, do not open the door until I return."

Donatella, however, was strong willed. As soon as her mother had walked just out of sight, Donatella started up the road. "Where are you walking to?" asked the people from her village whom she passed along the road.

"I am going to help my mother carry her burden back from the marketplace," she replied, hurrying past.

Soon Donatella encountered an elderly man slowly making his way down the road. He was a kind old man who was a close friend of Donatella and her mother. Donatella was so fond of him that she called him Grandfather even though they were not related.

"Hello, Grandfather," she said.

"Donatella, where are you going in such a rush?"

"I am going to meet up with mother and help carry our wares back from the marketplace."

"Then let me travel with you until you catch up with your mother."

"No, thank you," said Donatella, who was afraid he would discover that she was disobeying her mother. "Mother is just ahead of me on the road. I will run up and meet her." With that, she ran off.

Donatella kept just far enough behind her mother so that she could not be seen. Whenever her mother turned around, Donatella hid among the trees, wild vines and brambles that lined the road.

In this way, she followed her mother into the land of the evil ogre. Becoming more and more afraid, Donatella hid in the deep shadows. But when she came around the next bend in the road her mother was now so far ahead that she could not see her. Donatella was all alone on the lonely, desolate road.

"Mother must have entered the woods," she thought. Indeed, her mother had walked off the road to avoid the ogre's house. Once past the house, Donatella's mother again found the road and continued toward the marketplace.

Donatella picked and stumbled her way through prickly brush and into the thick woods until she became hopelessly lost. To the little girl, the dark, twisted branches were like arms that might reach out to catch her. She called out for her mother, but she was too far away to be heard. Lonely and afraid, she sat down on a small patch of moss and began to cry.

Suddenly, as if from nowhere, a little boy dressed in crimson clothes appeared before her. This little boy was really an evil *sanguenell*—an elf who had worked his magic so that he appeared to Donatella as a small boy about her age. Through his spell, Donatella could not see an elf wearing a pointed hat and shoes with sharp, curled toes.

"Please, please tell me how I can get home!" pleaded Donatella. "I have lost my way."

"Do not worry, my friend," said the elf with a friendly smile. "There is a hilltop we can go to where your mother will find you on her way home. Come, follow me."

At first, Donatella hesitated because she was frightened, but the elf promised her all kinds of sweets, treats and games to play when they arrived. Then he pointed to a little house atop a high, steep hill.

"Hold my hand," said the elf. As soon as Donatella took the elf's hand, as if by a special power, the two of them were standing on top of the hill.

With the same power of illusion that the elf appeared to Donatella as a little boy, the small house seemed to be trimmed with glittering jewels and candies in every color of the rainbow.

When they walked in through the door, toys lay all around on the floor. Donatella believed she was really eating sweets and playing games with a little boy. The elf, however, was preparing her for the time when she would become so hungry that she would be willing to do anything for food. Then, she would be given to the other elves and the evil ogre.

"Eat as many treats as you like," said the elf. "Have you ever seen so many toys? You can play with them all. Your mother will be back to get you on her way home." Soon Donatella was having so much fun that she lost track of time and forgot all about where she was.

By now, Donatella's mother had returned home to find the girl missing. She ran door to door through the village to ask if anyone had seen her daughter. The villagers were surprised to see her so upset.

"This morning we saw Donatella on the road, and she said that she was following you to the marketplace. So we let her go."

"Surely there must be some evil afoot in the land," someone said. Everyone worried about what might happen to sweet Donatella.

All of the men and women of the village who did not have young children of their own to watch set out along the road to search for the missing girl. They looked everywhere between the village and the marketplace as the sun dipped low in the western sky. The search was called off when the stars came out and flickered overhead, but the townsfolk promised Donatella's mother that they would continue to look for Donatella at sunrise.

Throughout the next day the search party scoured the woods bordering the road to the neighboring village, but they found no sign of Donatella. The girl's mother was so heartbroken and overcome with grief that she lay in her bed and would not eat. All through the second night she grew weaker and more forlorn.

In the morning, for a third time, the villagers set out to search for Donatella. The old man whom Donatella called Grandfather remembered that there was a small house on top of a steep hill not far from the place along the road where Donatella was last seen. With his slow, steady gait, he climbed the steep slope to the house.

The crimson elf, when he saw the old man climbing the hill, whispered to Donatella, "Hide! An evil giant is coming to get you!" Donatella hid under some old woolen blankets stored in a chest tucked amid the shadows of the little house.

When the old man finally reached the front of the house, he placed his ear up to the door, held his breath and listened. It was absolutely still inside. As he opened the door, it creaked on its hinges and a bright ray of sunshine flooded the dark, dusty house, which looked as if it was empty. The old man brushed cobwebs from his face as he entered the door. He searched for any clue that would show Donatella had been there.

Donatella, as it turns out, was allergic to wool. Try as she might, she could not keep from sneezing where she lay hidden in the chest. As soon as the old man heard her sneezes, he walked over to the chest, opened it and found Donatella wrapped in the wool blankets.

Although she looked tired and thin, the old man was overjoyed to see Donatella. He picked her up and gave her a warm hug. "My prayers have been answered. You are all right! We have been looking everywhere for you these past few days. What are you doing hiding in these blankets while the town is roaming the countryside searching for you?"

"Grandfather!" she cried. "I am so glad it's you. I thought you were an evil giant. Where is mother?"

"She is home worried sick that you might never be found."

"But I have only been here a little while," she said. "The little boy who was dressed in the red clothes told me that mother would come for me very soon."

"A little while, you say? We have been searching for you for more than two days! I think you have caused your mother enough worry. Come with me, and let's get you home. Where is this little boy dressed in red? And what is this talk about an evil giant?"

"But I don't want to go! I like it here. I have all the toys, cookies and sweets I could ever want." As Donatella looked around the little house, however, she saw that the sun shone on nothing but a small, dark, unkempt room. "Where is he?" she asked anxiously. "Where is the little boy dressed in red? He was just here, and he said that you were an evil giant and that I should hide from you. Where have all the toys gone?"

The old man now understood just how much danger Donatella had been in. As quickly as his ancient legs would move, he carried her down the hill and all the way home.

"Donatella!" cried her mother when they came through the door of her bedroom. "Praise God that you are alive!" Even in her weakened state, Donatella's mother rose from bed, took the girl in her arms and smothered her with joyful kisses. "Look how thin you have become, child. What has happened to you? Where have you been?"

Donatella's mother gave her a warm bath and a meal of bread and hearty soup. As she was bathing and eating, Donatella began to tell her mother the story of her experience with the crimson elf, the little house, the sweets and toys, and how what she thought was going to be an evil giant turned out to be Grandfather. Her mother listened attentively, then said, "There will be time for you to tell the whole story later. For now, you must get some rest." She put Donatella to bed, and the girl fell into a long, deep sleep.

Once Donatella regained her strength, Grandfather came to visit and told her about the crimson elf and the ogre, and of how much danger the girl had been in from the moment she set out to follow her mother. Donatella then understood that there were forces in the world much more powerful than she. From that day on, Donatella always listened to what her mother said. She obeyed her requests to stay close to home and did not try to follow along on her mother's journeys.

By the light of the full moon, Leonora was a vision.

THE GOLDEN STONE

Many years ago there lived a king who had a handsome son named Francesco. The king loved his son dearly and wished him to be happy. But the king would not allow Francesco to make his own choices. "You will do as I tell you and marry whom I decide because I know what is best for you," said the king.

Francesco loved all things that were wild. He took long walks in the countryside listening to the birds, smelling the flowers and traveling the fields, forests and shores to enjoy nature in all its splendor. While on those journeys, Francesco met many common folk and loved to visit with them. He admired these good-hearted, hard-working people. In time, Francesco came to believe that with people, as well as in nature, all are equal whether they live in a palace or on a farm. Even though his father was so conscious of class and position in society, the boy promised himself that he would marry for love, no matter what the king said.

Some distance from the palace of the king and his son, a family of peasants worked hard on their land to grow food. They had a small, well-kept farm with fields, pasture and many fruit trees. This family grew most of the food they needed to live, wove their own cloth for clothes and traded goods to others for the few things they could not make.

It was a greater struggle for this family than most, though, because there was only a husband, a wife and their daughter Leonora. They made a mighty effort just to plow, sow and grow enough food to survive. Much of their land went fallow simply because it was too much work for them to grow crops there.

One spring, the farmer decided to cultivate some new fields. "This way," he thought, "we will be able to sell more than usual, and we can save for the day when Leonora has a family of her own." His daughter helped with the hard work of breaking the sod, removing the rocks and tilling the soil.

In the heat of the midday sun, as Leonora was turning over the soil, the girl's shovel struck a large stone. She began to dig around it and found that it was enormous. "Father, please come and help me move this large stone." The two of them cleared a hole around the rock and used some long poles to lever it out of the ground. This took a great effort because it was much heavier than they expected. With so much work still to do that day, they rolled the stone out of the way and did not pay much attention to it. After filling in the hole, they continued with the clearing and tilling.

At the end of the day, when the sun was low over the horizon, its orange and red hues played and danced across the sky. Leonora and her father finished their work and sat on the large stone to rest and enjoy the sunset before walking home for dinner.

As she was standing to leave, Leonora saw something glitter. "Father," she said, "see how the sunlight reflects off the stone where we have scratched it. This stone is the very color of the sunset."

"Yes, it is beautiful," her father agreed.

"This is not an ordinary stone," Leonora continued. "I have seen beauty like this very few times. It is the color of the scepter in the church. This stone looks as if it is solid gold."

"Nonsense!" said her father. "It is just a stone, although it does seem to reflect the sunlight brightly, like no stone I have ever seen. Let us ask our neighbors to give us their opinion. I will bring the oxcart and a ramp. We can load the stone and take it home."

Using the poles and the ramp, Leonora and her father were able, with much effort, to roll the stone into the oxcart, which lumbered over the rutted road that led from the newly cleared field to their modest farmhouse.

The neighboring farmers marveled at Leonora's find. "It does indeed look like gold," they said. "You are surely one of the most wealthy families in the kingdom!" Still the farmer, who had been extremely poor all his life, could not appreciate that he and his wife and child may now be wealthy beyond their most abundant dreams.

Like the golden rays of the rising sun moving across Earth, news of the farmer's newfound wealth spread throughout the land.

"How could this be?" demanded the king. "I cannot allow a farmer to claim for his own any gold found within the borders of my kingdom. The golden stone belongs to me."

"Father, no!" protested the prince. "This farmer and his daughter found the golden stone and dug it from the ground with their own hard work and sweat. It is rightfully theirs."

"Never!" screamed the king. "Peasants cannot be allowed such wealth."

"I am going to see for myself," said Francesco. He ran from the palace and flew down the road toward the peasants' farm.

Meanwhile, all of the farmers in the kingdom heard that the king intended to claim the golden stone for his own. These farmers wrote and signed a letter of protest warning the king that he would forfeit his share of that year's crops, and would face a rebellion, if he tried to take the golden stone from the farmer.

When the prince arrived at the farmer's house to see the stone, he found that the king's soldiers were already there demanding the golden stone. The prince himself signed the petition to the king and sided with the farmers. At this turn of events, and because he did not want to face an open revolt throughout the kingdom, the king reluctantly allowed the farmer to keep the golden stone.

Francesco, however, had found something greater than gold at the farm. He discovered the farmer's lovely daughter, Leonora. Soon, the prince returned to the farm and asked to see the golden stone once more. He had really come back because he wished to talk with Leonora. After their first meeting, the prince thought that, besides being more beautiful than he had remembered, Leonora was a sensitive girl with a kind heart. He was falling in love.

Over the coming months, the prince returned again and again to visit the farmer's daughter. In time, he was sure of his love for Leonora and came to see that she had, in turn, fallen in love with him.

One day, Francesco and Leonora were out walking and they reached the top of a hill from which there was a magnificent view of the land. The prince faced the girl, took her hands and said, "I love you with all my heart. It would make me happy beyond words if you would become my wife."

"I have hoped that one day you might ask that question," she replied. "You know that my heart belongs to you alone. There is nothing in the world that I want more than to spend my life with you. But you are a prince, and I am the daughter of a simple farmer."

"Those things do not matter to me," replied Francesco. "I vowed long ago that I would marry the woman I loved, no matter what her place in life. The joy I feel when I am with you brings me riches far greater than all the gold in the world."

Upon hearing these words, Leonora threw her arms around the prince and they shared their first kiss. When they returned to the farm to tell the girl's family, her father and mother were delighted.

As Francesco walked home that evening, he decided to properly introduce Leonora to his father. He hoped that the king, seeing how beautiful she was and how sincere their love for one another was, would consent and give his approval to their marriage.

The following morning, Francesco returned to Leonora's house with an elegant dress for her to wear when she visited the palace for the first time. "Please put on this dress. I want you to come to my home and meet my father."

When they arrived at the palace, Francesco introduced the king to his beloved. "Father, I would like you to meet Leonora, the woman I love and who has made me the happiest man in the kingdom by agreeing to become my wife. We would like to ask your blessing on our marriage."

"What!" shouted the king. "That is impossible! Have you forgotten who you are? This marriage is out of the question."

"I understand your beliefs about such matters, Father, but I have always known that I would marry for love and not for position. You leave me no choice. In order to follow my heart, I must give up my claim to the throne and begin a new life as a peasant."

No matter how much the king wished his son to marry a princess, he did not want to lose the boy forever. Deep in thought, he paced the floor for some time.

"Very well," he answered at last. "I will consent to this marriage. But you must allow me to present a formal welcome to your future wife. Once she returns to her home, I will send a messenger who will invite her to the palace with a letter. You shall have my blessing on this marriage when she follows every instruction contained in that letter."

Although Francesco and Leonora were concerned about what the king might ask of her, they were also relieved that he had changed his mind. "Do not worry," said the prince as they rode in his carriage back toward the farmhouse. "We will not allow anything to come between us."

When the letter of invitation arrived, however, the girl was so downhearted that she wept softly as she read it.

> You are invited to the palace, but you may not come hungry nor after a meal, you may not come naked nor wearing clothes, you may not come barefoot nor wearing shoes, you may not come in a carriage nor on foot, and you may not come at night nor during the day.

"Mother," said Leonora, "look at this invitation. What can I do? These conditions seem to be impossible! Am I ever to marry the prince?"

As her mother read the invitation, she began to smile. "The king is crafty indeed. But there are ways that we can do even those things that would seem could not be done."

Leonora listened carefully to her mother. "Since you cannot have eaten and must not be hungry, you will fast before your journey but will drink the juice of our sweetest grapes before you arrive. Because you must not go to the palace wearing clothes nor wearing none, you will wear my wedding veil, which we will wrap around you as a cover along with your long, thick, beautiful hair. Your feet will not be bare—in place of shoes you will put on my beautiful silk slippers. The king has said that you must not walk nor ride in a carriage, so you will travel on horseback. And your journey will be timed so that you arrive at the palace at dawn, in the brief moment just before the sun rises. When you knock on the king's door it will no longer be night, and it will be just before the break of day."

It was late into the night before Leonora was ready to make her journey to the palace. Stepping carefully, her horse slowly made its way along the road by the light of the full moon. Leonora was a vision silhouetted against the lunar orb. Her long hair and veil wrapped around her were gently blowing in the cool night breeze. She looked as though she and the horse, with its flowing mane and tail, were one.

In the early morning hour, all was still in the palace. When the sun glowed golden just below the eastern horizon, the sound of the voice of the great gold knocker on the palace door broke the stillness. Francesco, who had been hoping and waiting with anticipation for the arrival of Leonora, ran and opened the door.

Francesco invited Leonora to enter the palace. He stood speechless, gazing at her beauty. Soon, the king came down the great staircase asking, "Who would come calling at this hour before the day has even begun?" Then, he drew back as he saw Leonora standing before him.

"How did you get here?" the king asked Leonora.

"I came by horseback," Leonora replied.

"Are you hungry?"

"No, I have been fasting, but I drank of the sweetest grape juice from our vineyard along the way."

Slowly, a smile came over the king's face. He was pleased to see how Leonora had matched wits with him and met every condition described in his invitation.

"Well, Father?" inquired Francesco.

"Let the wedding proceed with my grateful blessing!" exclaimed the king. "Leonora will make a fine queen indeed. Preparations will begin at once!"

Leonora was dressed in a silken wedding gown, and the palace was decorated in exquisite finery. When all was ready, and once Leonora's mother and father had arrived, they all walked down to the palace gardens. That evening, by the glowing rays of a fiery sunset, Leonora and Francesco became husband and wife.

After the wedding, the prince and princess lived contentedly in the palace. The king came to love Leonora as his own child. Leonora's mother and father, although they were extremely wealthy because of the golden stone, returned to live on their farm, which was still their true home.

From that day on, the king understood what his son's belief meant, that every person is equal no matter what the value of the things they own in the world or the standing of the parents they were born to. He became a benevolent king who shared his wealth and his good nature openly with the farmers and all who lived in the surrounding lands.

Out of an ancient hollow tree stepped a wizened old man.

A Mountain of Contentment

There once lived a husband and wife who had three sons, Alberto, Nicolo and Domenico. Theirs was a difficult life. Although they worked hard, they often went without food or money.

Alberto, the firstborn son, journeyed out into the world to find a job so he could buy food for the family. He knocked on the door of the cobbler in town and asked, "Kind sir, I am a good worker who is willing to do any task. My family is hungry, and I wish to earn money with which to buy food. Do you have any work for me?"

"I am sorry. Times are slow, and I do not need any more help than I already get from my own sons."

Alberto visited the butcher and the baker, the farmer and the merchant, but he was unable to find work.

Then he came to the door of a house that was tucked deep in the forest. This house was strange for it was an ancient hollow tree. The windows and the peephole in the door were knotholes. Alberto knocked on the heavy door and a voice answered that seemed to come from a hollow branch sticking out of the trunk.

"Who goes there?"

"It is I, Alberto."

"What do you want?"

"I have come seeking work so that I can help feed my parents and brothers."

Out stepped a wizened old man with a floppy hat, furry eyebrows and a white beard that reached down to his knees. He was leaning on a crooked, knotted cane. A small owl was perched on his shoulder.

"Very well," he said to Alberto. "My horse is tethered to that tree. Ride him to the north, and you will come to a tall mountain that reaches past the clouds. Climb that mountain and give this letter to the woman who lives in the cottage at the summit. Once she has read the letter, ask for her response and bring it here to me."

Alberto turned to see a magnificent white horse saddled and waiting for him. In no time, the boy spurred the horse toward the mountains in the north. He rode through thick, dark forests, forded many rivers and streams and finally entered the foothills. After a long journey, just as the sun was setting, the white horse halted at the base of the steep slope of a very tall mountain.

The horse made a start to climb the dizzying slope, but Alberto hesitated and pulled back on the reins. "This mountain is impossible," he thought. "Look how its peak lies beyond the clouds. How could we climb such a slope without falling and getting badly hurt, or even killed? I will have to return the horse to the old man for I cannot go on."

Alberto traveled throughout the night by the light of the moon. Upon returning at sunrise to the tree where the old man lived, he knocked on the door.

"Who knocks on my door at this hour?" came the response.

"It is I, Alberto."

"And what news do you have from the woman on the mountaintop?"

"The mountain is impossibly steep. It cannot be climbed, so I have come to thank you and return your horse."

"Because you lack faith, I cannot help you," said the old man as he opened the door. "Leave the letter with me and return to your home where they can take care of you."

Alberto walked sadly home. When he told his family about his adventure, they were disappointed.

"Hah!" said Nicolo. "You have never believed in yourself. I will go and climb that mountain without fail. Where can I find this old man?"

Nicolo followed the route that his brother had taken. In time, he came to the old tree just as Alberto had described it.

"Old man," cried Nicolo as he knocked on the door, "I wish to speak with you."

"Who goes there?"

"It is I, Nicolo, at your service."

"What do you want?"

"I have come to complete the task that my brother Alberto could not. My family is poor, and we need food to eat. Can you help me?"

Out came the old man leaning on his twisted cane.

"You must deliver this letter by horseback to the woman who lives on top of the tall mountain in the north. Climb up above the clouds and knock on the door to the cottage. Present the letter to the woman who lives there. She will give you a message in return, which you are to bring to me. Now take my horse and go. Do not delay."

"As you wish, good sir."

All day Nicolo drove the white horse toward the land of the cold winds. At last, he made his way through the foothills. Finally, the magnificent peak stood before him. The horse chomped at the bit and anxiously pawed the ground, so eager was it to climb the steep slope toward the clouds that enshrouded the summit.

"Look at those jagged rocks," said Nicolo to the horse. "How easily they could come loose and send us plummeting. A horse cannot climb such a slope. I fear that we would both fall to our deaths."

By the light of the moon and stars, Nicolo led the horse over the hills, across the rivers, through the deep woods and back to the old man's tree. Nicolo found the old man sitting on a gnarled root and leaning on the trunk of the ancient tree.

"What news do you have from the mountaintop?" he asked Nicolo.

"Sir, I did not climb the mountain."

"Why not?" inquired the elder impatiently.

"The slope was at such an incline I feared we would both fall to our deaths," responded Nicolo.

"Give me the letter and go home where your family can keep you safe from the dangers of the world! I can be of no help. You have allowed fear to defeat you."

Nicolo rode dejectedly home and, at last, entered his own yard where the family was waiting.

"Welcome, Nicolo," said his father. "Did you find some work? Have you brought us some bread to eat?"

"No father," replied Nicolo. "I am sorry." Then he told his family the story of what had happened.

"Domenico," said the father turning to his third son. "You are our last hope."

"But Domenico is the youngest of us all," protested Alberto and Nicolo. "How can he succeed where we have failed? Brother, it would be better if you stayed home and helped mother with her chores," they said mockingly.

"You have had your chance to help," said Domenico, who would not be swayed. "It is my turn, and I am going to do my best." Although Domenico was young, he was brave and quick-witted. He implored his brothers to give him directions to the old man's house in the hollow tree. Finally, they relented and told him the way.

On and on walked Domenico until, and at last, he stood on the threshold of the old man's house and knocked.

"Who would knock on my door?" asked a voice that seemed to come from the tree itself.

"With all respect, sir, it is I, Domenico."

"And what do you wish?"

"My family is hungry and without money to buy food. Is there some work that you could give me so that we would be able to buy food to eat?"

"Indeed," answered the old man as he slowly opened the door of his house. So stooped was he with age that he was barely taller than Domenico. "On top of a tall, steep mountain in the north there lives a wise woman. The head of this mountain reaches above the clouds. Ride my horse to the mountain and climb to the top. Then, knock on the door of the cottage there and give this letter to the woman who answers."

"Thank you," said Domenico as he carefully took the letter from the old man's hand. In the blink of an eye, Domenico nimbly leapt onto the back of the white horse and galloped away toward the mountain in the north. They rode through the dense forests, across the rushing rivers and into the foothills until, at last, he and the horse stood gazing up at the clouds that ringed the summit of the mountain.

Domenico could feel the horse's great desire to climb the mountain. "This is the time of our truth," he said to the horse. "Up with you now, climb to your heart's content."

At that, the horse bounded up the steep, rocky slope with ease, its hooves clopping along the cobbles and outcroppings. In a short time, their heads were hidden in the soft whiteness of the clouds near the summit. To Domenico's surprise, horse and rider climbed through the clouds and came out into bright sunlight that shimmered green against the lush grass of a beautiful pasture. Although there was enough grass growing there to feed a great herd of cattle, the cattle that Domenico saw grazing were thin and sickly.

On they rode through the herd, who were too weak and listless to heed them. At last they saw the small cottage ahead, surrounded by a poor, rocky pasture from which grew sparse clumps of grass. Domenico's eyes widened in amazement as he noticed that the cattle feeding there were plump and healthy.

At last, Domenico stood before the door of the cottage and knocked. Instantly, the door flew open and there stood a tall, lean woman with a wreath the colors of the rainbow wrapped around her head. Her hair was the hue of the night sky. A thousand stars seemed to sparkle in her eyes, and her skin was the gold of the harvest moon. She was carrying a long shepherd's crook. The curve at the top was made from a ram's horn carved into the shape of the crescent moon.

"Who are you, and why have you come to this place?" she asked Domenico.

"There is an old man who lives in a hollow tree a great distance away in the south. Here is the letter that he asked me to deliver to you," said Domenico as he handed it to her.

"Well done!" she replied. "I have been waiting a long time for this letter. You are a remarkable young man."

With that she took the letter from his hand and read it carefully.

"Here is my response to the old man," she said. "The bony cattle who graze in the lush, rich fields are consumed with hunger. Although they are surrounded with more than enough food to feed them all, they constantly fight with one another over who has the greenest and tastiest grass to eat. Their greed, envy and jealousy have made them sick and weak with hunger even as they live in the midst of riches. Beyond these pitiful animals lives the herd of cattle who grow strong and healthy in the poorest of pastures. There, where little tufts of grass grow in between the rocks and gravel, these cattle have grown hearty and content because they make the most of the scant food that Earth has given them."

Domenico thanked the strange woman and rode the horse as quickly as it could travel down the dangerous slope, over the foothills, across the rivers and through darkest wood until he reached the house of the old man. There he found the gnarled one, seated on a log as if he were expecting Domenico at that precise moment.

"Good sir, I have a message from the woman who lives on the mountaintop in the land to the north." Domenico told the old man all that he had seen and heard. A smile came to the old man's face.

"Your faith and courage have served you well. You will be rewarded with food for your family and wisdom that will serve you throughout your life. You will appreciate the gifts you receive and will be a truly happy man."

"Thank you with all my heart," said Domenico. "I will never forget what I have learned."

Then, Domenico started for home, anxious to tell his family of his great adventure. Never again did hunger visit their household. From that day forward, people journeyed great distances to seek Domenico's wise counsel.

A frog sat on the lily pad next to where Pietro's stone had come to rest.

FROG PRINCESS

Long ago a king and queen ruled over a peaceful land. The king and queen had three sons. In time these young men reached the age when each was ready to find a wife.

The king, however, did not want his sons to fight over whom they would marry.

"This is how it will be," said the king. "Take your slingshots and shoot a stone as far as you can. Wherever each stone lands, there you will find your wife."

The three young men were excited. Each, in turn, pulled back his slingshot as far as he could and let the stone fly.

The stone shot by the first son, Enrico, landed on the roof of the cobbler's shop. This son ran to the cobbler's door and knocked. When the door opened, there stood a pretty maiden with fine hair and fair skin. Enrico offered her a ring, and she gladly put it on.

When the stone shot by Antonio, the second son, came down, it flew through a window and plopped into a loaf of bread being kneaded by the baker. So it was that the baker's daughter, all sweetness and spice, became the wife-to-be of the second son.

Up and over the town went the stone shot by the third, youngest son, whose name was Pietro. After flying a great distance, this stone landed in a quiet pond where the water lilies grew. By the time Pietro reached the shore of the pond, night had fallen, and the moon was nearly full. In the glowing moonlight, the young man saw that a frog sat on the lily pad next to where his stone had come to rest.

The young prince was very disappointed. "Why did my stone have to land near a frog?" he asked himself. Still, Pietro was an honest young man who always respected his father's wishes. He resigned himself to the idea of taking a frog for a wife.

When Pietro returned home to the palace, he found his two brothers telling their parents about their good fortune.

"This is good news," said the queen. "Your father and I are getting old. One day a new king and queen will have to take our places."

"Which one of us would you choose?" asked Enrico.

"The one who finds the finest wife will become the future king!" the king replied. "And where did your stone land?" he asked his third son.

"It came to rest in a lily pond, next to a frog," answered the boy, who looked down at his feet and felt humiliated. His two brothers began to chuckle, but their father motioned them to be quiet.

At that, the king handed a ball of thread to each of his sons, saying, "I want each of you to come back to me in three days with the cloth that your future wife has spun from this thread."

Each son did as their father had asked. Pietro, however, felt strange as he stood on the shore of the pond. "Hello, Frog," he called.

The frog swam over to the shore and simply replied, "Yes, who are you?"

"I am Pietro, the king's third son."

"Do you love me?"

"No."

"No matter. One day you shall. What do you want of me?"

"Please," he asked her, "spin this thread into cloth. I will return in three days to see what you have made." The prince handed the ball of thread to the frog.

In time, Pietro returned to the pond and called, "Frog, it is me."

"Do you love me?"

"No."

"No matter. One day you shall." The frog then presented the young man with a walnut.

"What am I to do with this walnut?" he asked the frog as he looked at the walnut with a puzzled expression.

The frog replied, "Give the walnut to your father and ask him to open it."

When he arrived at the castle, Pietro was downhearted. The cobbler's daughter had woven a fine cloth for Enrico. When Antonio unfolded the fabric made by the baker's daughter, it felt as smooth as the fur of a newborn fawn.

Feeling foolish, Pietro gave the walnut to his father. "This is what the frog gave me after I presented her with the thread," he explained. "She said that you should open it." The other two sons laughed at the sight of the walnut.

As soon as the king split open the walnut, however, a great fold of silken cloth unfurled. More and more of this fine cloth came out of the shell as the king pulled on it. "This cloth must be enchanted," the king exclaimed. "It seems to go on forever." With those words, the king found himself holding the end of the cloth in his hands.

Clearly, the frog's cloth was the best of all. The king was not happy. "We cannot have a frog for a queen!" he thought to himself, although he did not share this feeling with his sons.

So the king thought of another task that the three wives-to-be should perform. He went into the castle and came out holding three puppies and gave one to each of his sons. "Give your intended one

of these puppies. Whoever takes the best care of her puppy between now and when the full moon returns, will be queen."

The three sons visited their wives-to-be and asked them to take
good care of the puppies. Patiently the two older brothers waited
and watched the many faces of the moon, which seemed to change
more slowly than usual. To Pietro, the moon seemed to move
through its cycle much quicker than he might have hoped. When
the moon was full once again, the three sons brought the puppies
back to the king.

The baker's daughter had fed her puppy so much that it was fat
and lazy. The puppy that was left with the cobbler's daughter had
not received enough attention, and its tail had stopped wagging.

Then, Pietro gave his father a tiny box. Inside the box the king
found a contented, well-groomed puppy that licked his face as he
held it up.

"So be it," the king said to his youngest son. "You shall be king,
and your frog wife will sit beside you on the throne of the queen."

"But father … ," Pietro began to say.

"I'm sorry, son, this is the way it must be." So the prince ac-
cepted his fate.

All three sons were to be married on the same day. Enrico and
Antonio called on their brides-to-be in brightly decorated carriages
pulled by the king's finest horses. The daughters of the cobbler and
baker were dressed in beautiful silks and wore flowers in their hair.

Back at the pond, Pietro found that the frog was ready. She rode
in a coach made of the leaf from a water lily. A beautiful water lily
flower sat atop the coach, which was pulled by a team of snails. Slowly,
the carriage inched toward the palace. The reluctant youth walked
ahead. He kept stopping to wait for the coach. Once, he walked so far
ahead that he lay down to wait and his eyes closed in slumber.

The sound of braying horses woke him with a start. There, in
front of the youth, stood a team of snow-white horses and a glorious

coach decorated with diamonds, rubies and other sparkling gems. A coachman sat at the reigns. When Pietro opened the door to look inside, he found a fair maiden upon a seat made of cloth as soft as a cloud. She was wearing a stunning silk gown the color of green leaves that shimmered in the sunlight.

"Do I know you?" he asked.

"Of course. You once saw me as a frog."

"How could that be?" he exclaimed with delight.

"Long ago I was Princess Isabella as you see me now. A curse was put upon me, and I was turned into a frog. Only if a king's son would agree to marry me as a frog could the spell be broken. By accepting our marriage, you have changed me back into a princess."

With that, Pietro climbed into the coach. In their joy, the couple embraced and kissed for the first time.

"Coachman," cried the youth, "to the palace!"

The king and his two other sons were waiting when the coach arrived at the palace. The door swung open, then the youngest son and his bride-to-be stepped out.

"But son, where is the frog?" asked the king.

"She was really the Princess Isabella, who had been placed under an evil curse," explained the prince. "The spell was broken when I agreed to make her my wife."

So pleased was the king that he took the maiden's hand and kissed it. "I would like to invite you, Princess Isabella, into our family." Then, the king turned to face his wife and sons as he proclaimed, "Let us welcome our future queen to her new home!"

"Don't you recognize me? You are looking into the face of Death."

THE LAND OF ETERNAL LIFE

Gennaro was only a boy when his grandmother passed away. He loved her very much, and it made him sad to think that she was gone. Her death scared the boy. "I don't ever want that to happen to me," he thought.

"Mother," he asked one day, "why do people have to die? Will it happen to all of us? Isn't there something we can do to live as long as we like?"

"Why are you dwelling on such a sad thing as death?" she answered.

"Because of Grandmother," said Gennaro.

"I know how you feel," said his mother. "I miss her, too. But, son, death is a part of life. Everyone dies when their time comes."

"No, it will never happen to me!" Gennaro exclaimed. "Some day," he thought, "I am going on a great journey to find the place where I will live forever."

A few years later, when Gennaro was a young man, he visited all his friends and relatives. "I wish to say good-bye. Today I am setting out to look for the place where I will live forever."

Gennaro walked to the next village, then the one after that. Through countryside where farms dotted the landscape, through cities and over bridges across great rivers he traveled. In each town he asked the people he encountered, "Do you know the way to the land where people live forever?" "What?" was the usual response. "Are you mad? There is no such place in all the world."

Gennaro continued on his journey toward the west, which led through the most beautiful farmland he had ever seen. He walked past waving fields of grain, pastures grazed by great herds of cattle and hillsides lined with rows of vineyards whose vines were heavy with grape. In the center of one friendly village, Gennaro stopped for lodging. The townsfolk were enjoying the annual harvest festival.

"Welcome," said the handsome man who ran the inn. "What brings you to our village? Have you come to enjoy our festival?"

"No," responded Gennaro. "I am on my way to find the land of eternal life."

"The what? Look around you, my son. You are surrounded by life as we speak."

"Yes, I can see that this is a wonderful festival. I plan to stay and enjoy it myself. But then I will continue on to find the place where I will never have to die."

"I tell you what," said the innkeeper. "Down in my wine cellar, I am aging a vintage made from the finest grapes we have ever grown in these parts. It will not be finished for many, many years. If you agree to watch these bottles of wine and turn them for me when they need it, you will live until the wine is ready."

"When will that be?"

"Not for another three or four generations," answered the man. "About one hundred years or so."

"Thank you for your kind offer, but where I am going, I will live forever."

Gennaro stayed in that village for two days. He enjoyed the generosity of those people and their joyous spirit. Then, he said good-bye to his new friends and walked off to the west.

From the side of the road, Gennaro saw an old woman in the forest who was planting trees on a mountainside. The young man stopped to watch her for a time. She was dressed in green, had a large sack draped over her shoulder and carried a staff that was pointed on the end. Nimble for her age, she went along and poked the end of the staff into the moist, brown earth and dropped a seed into each hole. Gennaro walked toward her.

"Can you tell me how to get to the land of eternal life?" he asked.

"No, I have never heard of such a place," she responded. "But if you stay with me and help plant these seeds, you will live as long as it takes to grow a great forest that will cover the slopes of this tall mountain."

"And how long is that?" asked Gennaro.

"It is a job for many lifetimes. It will take more than two hundred long years of hard work."

"What will happen when the job is finished?"

"Then we will have accomplished a great thing. Our time here on Earth will be over. We will both die."

"But I am looking for the land of eternal life, not someplace where I will live only two hundred years. I gratefully decline your offer and wish you good health and the best weather for growing your trees. Good-bye."

On walked Gennaro toward the setting sun. In time he came to a barren, desolate land where the sun shone long and hot each day. There he found an old man who was building a gigantic wall out of stones. The man was stooped from many years of bending over and picking up thousands of stones. He wore a stained, wide-brimmed hat to protect his head from the sun. A long beard, the color of the stones themselves, hung down almost to the ground.

"Kind sir," said Gennaro, "that is a magnificent wall. How long have you labored to build it?"

The man was glad to take a break from wall building to speak with Gennaro. "Greetings, young man. I have been building this wall for as long as I can remember, my entire lifetime."

"Why are you building such a tall, strong wall?"

"Many years ago, this was a rich and fertile land teeming with villages and cities of great wealth. Then, there was a war. Thousands of people were killed and their enemies laid waste to the land, cutting the trees and burning the fields until they created this Godforsaken place you see before us. The few survivors who live here still fight with their enemies when they meet. I am building this wall to keep them apart forever so that there may once again be peace, and the land may heal."

"That is the most tragic story I have ever heard. I, myself, am on a journey in search of a beautiful place, the land of eternal life. Do you, by chance, know where I could find it?"

"Why do you seek such a place?"

"Because I do not want to die," answered Gennaro.

"There is no place such as the one you describe. If, however, you remain with me and help build this wall, you will live until it is completed."

"And when will that be?"

"Three hundred years from now, at least."

"But I do not want to live for a mere three hundred years," Gennaro exclaimed. "When I find what I am looking for I will live forever. Thank you and may your wall bring the peace you hope for."

"Three hundred years is a long time to live," the old man insisted. "Nonetheless, I hope you find what you are seeking. Good-bye and safe journeys."

Gennaro walked quickly away from the old man. Glad to be leaving that barren, wounded land behind, he continued his journey to the west. Gradually, small springs appeared gurgling from the hillsides. Streams flowed down into rivers that meandered through the valleys. Trees and bushes that bore delicious nuts and wild berries grew along the riverbanks. Gennaro stopped often to drink the clean, clear water and to pick his meals from the branches. All around, the land unfolded in rolling hills covered with a carpet of grasses and flowers of many bright colors. Gennaro's spirit soared in these open spaces.

At last, in the distance, Gennaro heard a sound that he had only been told about in stories. He recognized it as the sound of waves breaking on the seashore. As he ran toward the sound, he noticed a spectacular palace sitting high up on a bluff overlooking the ocean. He went excitedly up to the door of the palace. The knocker was a large gold ring that Gennaro swung down against the ancient door. The sound echoed through the rooms of the palace within.

Slowly, the door opened and there stood a man who looked, to Gennaro, as if he might be very old, or might not be very old. He was tall, stood straight and his arms appeared strong and muscular. His hair was white as snow, and he had a long white beard, which waved in the ocean breeze blowing through the door. His eyes were the color of the sea, and they looked weary and worn.

"Good day!" bellowed the man. "It has been hundreds of years since I have had a visitor, and I am glad to see you!"

"Hello, good sir," replied Gennaro.

"Why have you come to my palace?"

"This is the end of a long journey," said Gennaro. "I am searching for something that may not even exist."

"And what do you seek?"

"The land of eternal life."

"Indeed! Here it is! Welcome," said the man. "Come in and see for yourself. If you remain here in the palace, you will have life everlasting."

"Then I have been rewarded for my long journey! Thank you for inviting me in, but how long may I stay?"

"As long as you wish. These have been lonely years in the palace, and I have been praying for companionship."

Gennaro began a life of splendor in the palace. The meals were abundant and delicious. Gennaro and his companion enjoyed each other's company. They played many games, and their conversations often went on well into the night.

There were lovely gardens on the palace grounds in which he loved to pass the time. Row upon row of interesting books lined the walls of the study. Gennaro spent many days lost in a world he discovered inside a new book. When he grew tired, he went for a walk in the refreshing sea air. But Gennaro could not walk down to the shore and touch the waves because he was forbidden to leave the palace grounds.

Year after year passed in this way, but Gennaro was so content that he had no idea how many years had gone by.

One day, Gennaro approached his companion. "I miss my family greatly and I would like to see them again. It is beautiful here in the palace, but my heart is calling for me to visit the place of my birth."

"That would not be possible. No one from your family is still alive. Even the countryside is greatly changed."

"But at least I could see my village, and the descendants of those I left behind."

"There is one way that you could do what you are asking, but it carries great risk."

"Please, tell me what I must do."

"Take my white horse. She moves as softly and swiftly as the sea breezes. Ride to the east toward your village. No matter what happens, you must remain in the saddle. If you step down from the horse, you will die instantly."

"Thank you," said Gennaro, then he flew out to the stable to saddle up the white horse. In no time he had mounted the horse, and the two of them set out across the lands that surrounded the palace. On they rode through a sea of grass and flowers, then under the branches of the nut trees that grew by the riverbanks.

In the distance Gennaro saw a gray ribbon snaking over the land. As he rode closer, he realized that it was the stone wall the old man had been building when Gennaro walked past him many years ago. Gennaro spurred the white horse on and followed the stone wall to the south, where it ended. There, resting against the finished end of the wall where the old man had sat down to rest when his work was completed, was a small heap of bones.

"Such as I would be if I had remained here to help build this wall," thought Gennaro.

On they rode until the land once again turned green. Gennaro saw a great mountain rising up in the east. Its once-barren slopes were now covered with a carpet of leaves. As they approached, Gennaro could see that the carpet was really a dense, beautiful forest. Upon entering the woods on the back of the white horse, Gennaro heard the sweet songs of birds in the treetops. Squirrels scurried through the leaves gathering nuts. A deer leapt from the brush, crossed the road and melted into the shadows.

"This is a magnificent forest," Gennaro thought. "The old woman who planted these trees has created life far greater than I could have ever imagined. She lives on in these trees."

Horse and rider emerged from the forest and followed the road toward the village in which Gennaro enjoyed the harvest festival long ago, and where he had stayed for a few nights at the invitation of the innkeeper. The lush farmland was still being worked, and the vineyards lined the hillsides. But the village had grown beyond its old boundaries, and there now stood a small city. In the center of that city, where Gennaro had once spent the night at the inn, there now stood a large stone building. Many people were employed in that building bottling wine made from the grapes grown in the surrounding vineyards. The winery was owned by the descendants of the old innkeeper.

"Employment for these people, and that delicious wine, is the fruit of the life of the innkeeper whom I once met here," Gennaro realized. "His joy and hard work have lived on, bringing good fortune and happiness to many thousands of people over the years."

Further along the road, Gennaro remembered the lush, green farmlands that lay ahead in the outskirts of his own village. As he approached, he entered a dark forest. The stone walls that used to separate pastures now lay in the shadows of the trees. When Gennaro entered the village, its streets were unfamiliar to him. The houses that he had known from boyhood were gone, including the one he had grown up in. Gennaro rode through the village and asked about his family and the families of his friends. But those family names were unknown to anyone in the village. So much had changed that it was as if Gennaro had never been born there.

Tears welled up in Gennaro's eyes. "How could things have been altered so completely?" he asked himself. "There is nothing left for me here."

Gennaro began the long journey back to the land of eternal life. On the way, he came upon an old man tugging at an oxcart that was piled high with many pairs of old, worn-out shoes.

"He must be a peddler," thought Gennaro.

"Dear boy," asked the old man. "My wheel has sunk into the mud and lodged against a stone. I cannot pull it free by myself. I would be most grateful if you would lend a hand."

"I am sorry, but that is not possible," said Gennaro.

"But there is no one else around to help me," continued the old man, "and I can feel the cold evening chill entering my bones even as we speak. I must be home by nightfall."

Gennaro, having a kind heart, could not stand to see the old man struggle with such a heavy load. Yet he knew that he would die if he stepped down to help the man pull his cart out of the mud. For a time, Gennaro sat frozen upon his horse, torn between remaining in the saddle and getting down. "Of what value will my life be," he thought, "if my heart must become cold and uncaring for me to continue living?"

Finally, Gennaro summoned his courage. He swung out of the saddle and stepped down. As soon as his foot touched the ground, the old man took hold of him and would not let go. Gennaro was afraid of the surprising strength in the old man's grip.

"Now you are mine!" he said.

"Who are you?" Gennaro demanded as he struggled to get loose. "Let go of me!"

"Don't you recognize me?" said the old man. "You are looking into the face of Death. Piled on my cart are all the shoes that I have worn out as I pursued you over great distances these many years. But now you are in my grasp, and it is impossible to break free."

And so, Gennaro never returned to the land of eternal life. It is often said, however, that he continued his journey. Although he lost his life in this world, Gennaro eventually found a far greater reward.

"Four sacks of gold. No less!" exclaimed the old woman.

BOOKS OF WISDOM

Once a great city sat in the middle of a fertile plain. The soil in the fields was rich, and there always seemed to be just the right amount of sunshine and rain. No one went hungry because the harvest was ever bountiful. The people of the city had flourished as far back as anyone could remember.

It was summer, and the people were out tending their crops in the fields when a haggard old woman labored across the plain pulling a large wooden cart behind her. She drew near to the city, and the curious followed her in through the gate.

A crowd gathered around the old woman as she pulled her cart into the center of the city square. Twelve leatherbound books were stacked neatly in the cart. The people marveled at these magnificent books which were of great age and decorated with beautiful designs.

One of the city elders stepped forward. "Welcome to our city," he said. "Perhaps you will be so kind as to tell us why you have come here. We can see that you are bearing something of importance in your cart."

"I have here in this cart twelve books," croaked the old woman. "They contain all of the knowledge and all of the wisdom of the world."

"And why have you brought them here to us?" he asked.

"I will sell them to you if you want them."

"And what price are you asking?"

"You may have all twelve of these books for one sack of gold," she replied.

"One sack of gold! Old woman, gold is clearly worth far more than you think it is. We are not interested in buying your old books for a sack of gold."

With that, the townsfolk pointed the way back toward the city gate.

"Very well," said the old woman. But before she left, she lit a fire and threw six of the old books upon the flames. Once these books had been destroyed, she rolled her cart back through the gate of the city and out across the plains.

It was a pretty good year for the people of the city. Crops were not as abundant as usual, but they still produced a good harvest. There was just enough food to last through the winter and spring.

When the old woman returned again late the following spring-time, the crops were already growing. Again she attracted a crowd as she rolled her cart of ancient books into the city square.

"Welcome," said one of the village elders. "We were wondering if we would see you again. What are you offering us now?"

"I have in this cart six books. They contain one-half of all of the knowledge and one-half of all the wisdom of the world," replied the old woman. "I would be glad to sell them to you."

"Yes, yes, I am sure you would. And what are you asking for these six books now?" the elder inquired.

"Two bags of gold."

"Surely you must be joking!" said the elder. "You come into our city offering half of the twelve books at twice the price. Do you take us for fools?"

"Then you do not wish to buy the books?"

"No! We work hard for our wages and will not pay such an outrageous sum!"

"As you wish," said the old woman.

She gathered some sticks, built them into a pile and lit them. Then she placed three more of the books upon the fire. When the books were ablaze, the old woman turned her cart around and left the village.

It was a disastrous year for the people of the city. For the first time in memory, the rains did not come. Many of the crops were ruined by the drought. The meager harvest left many people weak with hunger after the bitter winter. An illness swept through the city. Some people did not live to see the birds return from the south.

That spring, as the people were out planting their crops, they kept watching for the old woman. One day, after the seeds had begun to sprout, someone cried out, "Here she comes. Look, there to the east!"

The old woman rolled her cart back to the center of the city square.

"Welcome, old woman," said one of the city elders. "We did not expect you until later in the season."

"Indeed," she cackled, "I am moving more quickly these days. There are only three books left to pull."

"These books contain one-fourth of all the knowledge and one-fourth of all the wisdom of the world."

"What are you asking for your books now?" someone yelled.

"Four sacks of gold."

"Old woman!" the elder cried out in alarm. "Every time you come to offer us your books you have less of them, and yet you ask for more gold. As you know, things are not well in our city, and we were hoping that your books would be of help to us. But we will not pay such an unreasonable price just because we are going through a hard time."

"Very well," she said with a faint smile on her face, "then I will need some firewood."

"No, wait!" a woman pleaded. "This is not helping anyone. You are burning up the books you want to sell us, and we are not getting any wiser. Give us some time to talk this over."

So the elders held a meeting. After a few hours of discussing and arguing among themselves, they came back to reason with the old woman.

"This is what we have decided. We are going to read the remaining three books. If we find that the knowledge and wisdom they contain is of value, then we will offer you an appropriate sum."

"Four sacks of gold. No less!" exclaimed the old woman.

"And if we refuse?" the elders asked.

"Then books will burn."

"We will not give you one stick of firewood!" they shouted.

"I do not need your help," she said.

With that, she knelt down, tore the pages from one of the remaining books and crumpled them into a pile. After she lit these pages and they were burning brightly, she threw one of the last two books upon the flames and watched until both books had been consumed. Finally, she turned her cart around and left the village in haste.

Later, by the light of the moon when the city was asleep, some of the people sneaked into the town square. Carefully they combed through the ashes that remained of the two books of wisdom that had been burned. They searched for a fragment of unburnt paper in hopes of discovering a morsel of the knowledge and wisdom that the old woman had offered them. Alas, the books had been completely destroyed by the flames.

The following winter was even harder than the one before. As springtime grew near, the people of the city were anxious for the old woman to arrive. Plans were made to give her a warm welcome. Watchers were posted to keep an eye to the eastern horizon.

One day, in late spring, the horns sounded from the watchtowers near the village gate. "She comes!" shouted the watchers. "The old woman is approaching with her cart!"

The old woman was surprised at how glad the people of the city were to see her. She thanked them for their welcome as she rolled the cart with the single leatherbound book upon it into the city square.

"You are most welcome!" the townsfolk said. "We are happy to see you."

"As you can see, I now have only one book left in this cart," she said. "There was even enough room for some firewood. This book contains one-twelfth of all the knowledge and one-twelfth of all the wisdom of the world."

"Yes, we know," said one of the village elders. "And we have budgeted a certain sum for the purchase of this book based on what you have asked in the past. Now, how much do you want for that book?"

"Sixteen sacks of gold!" demanded the old woman.

"But … but we gathered eight sacks of gold because you have doubled your price every time you returned. This is all of the gold that we have in the city treasury! We cannot possibly afford sixteen sacks of gold."

"Sixteen sacks of gold," she repeated, "or … " Then she knelt down and began to sing under her breath as she arranged the wood for a fire.

"Stop!" cried the people of the city. "We will find a way to meet your price."

Everyone who lived in the city searched their personal belongings for gold jewelry, gold goblets and other family treasures and heirlooms. Everything that was made of gold in the entire city was brought to the treasury and placed in sacks. When this was done, the sum of all the wealth of the people of the city filled exactly sixteen sacks.

These sacks were rolled into the center of the square on two carts pulled by oxen and presented to the old woman. She thanked the people of the city and gave them the one remaining leatherbound book.

"We hope this book is worth the price!" the people exclaimed.

"Oh yes, it is, and then some," said the old woman. "You cannot even imagine what wonders were contained in the other eleven books."

Then, the old woman guided the oxcarts that held the sixteen sacks of gold out through the city gates across the plain. With heavy hearts, the people of the city watched her trail of dust until it disappeared over the western horizon.

The old woman never returned. Those people struggled on and did their best to live with only one-twelfth of all of the knowledge and one-twelfth of all of the wisdom that once existed in the world.

To this day, all the people of the world are on a great journey. We are still trying to find the knowledge and wisdom that was lost when those eleven books were burned long ago. Whenever we act wisely, we rediscover a bit of truth and the world becomes a better place for our children and all the children to come.

Author's Note to Parents, Teachers and Librarians

Sharing the Tales

The Crimson Elf: Italian Tales of Wisdom presents my original tellings of traditional folktales and fairy tales from Italy. I have considered hundreds of tales in my search to find those that address matters that are important to children growing up in our time. Although these tales come from the provinces of ancient Italy, their wisdom is fresh and speaks to children of all ages.

While many Italian fairy tales are influenced by the medieval period, in general, Italian folktales are not as violent as tales from many European countries. There is, however, a dark side to some Italian tales such as "The Crimson Elf" and "The Land of Eternal Life." Often, these tales tell of dying or being eaten. This darkness, however, is a place from which to grow and change, from which to overcome the evil impulses that we all feel at times and transform our lives to become a force for good in the world. An individual learns to look outside of her or his life to help others. It is this movement from darkness into light that gives many folktales their moral strength.

In my retellings, I have kept the original heart of each story. The meaning, the message and the feel of the original tales remain. In this book I take the same approach that I use in my role as a storyteller who draws on tales from many different cultures. I work with a story until it becomes a part of me. At that point the story speaks to me, and I can hear the voices of the characters who live in the story. I am then able to create an original telling of the tale that includes the parts of the story that bring it to completion.

How can you—parents, teachers, librarians and other adults—best share these stories with children? Children can read them in quiet solitude, or someone can read the stories aloud and share them with others. You can help children experience these stories on many levels. Taken literally, the stories are pure entertainment. Look deeper into the lives and events found in these tales and discover that they are a rich source of folk wisdom and truth. The stories speak to people of different ages and places in life because we each bring our unique selves, our thoughts and feelings, into the story as we experience it. These Italian tales expand our horizon and deepen our understanding of life. They show us that, down through the ages, the experience of living in the natural world and growing in human community is timeless and universal.

ITALIAN STORYTELLING IN AMERICA

In modern Italy, storytelling has moved from the stable to the kitchen or parlor, wherever there is food, the warmth of a stove and the good company of family and friends. This is also true with many Italian-American families. Today, in place of a traditional storyteller who brings folktales to life, families often share stories of past poverty, hardship and epic migrant journeys to America. Whenever someone describes the old country, it is often as an idealized place where people lived close to the land and shared a deep relationship with God.

In my family, as I was growing up, I heard many stories from my mother, my father and my paternal grandmother. Over the years, these simple tales became our family myths. My grandmother, Anna (Durante) Caduto, who was born on 28 March 1902, often tells stories of growing up in the village of Pietravairano, a small village that covers a hillside and valley in the northwest corner of the province of Campania. When I visited my relatives in Pietravairano in September 1990, I found myself in a landscape that, as a child, I heard described to me hundreds of times. This experience was nothing less than walking through a mythic place guided by people from a fairy tale come to life.

Most of the stories that my father, Ralph, tells are family stories. My grandmother and my mother, Esther (Martone) Caduto, however, have told me several traditional tales from the region around Pietravairano. One of the most interesting is the story of Saint Eraclio. High up on the hillside, overlooking Pietravairano, is the lovely church of Saint Eraclio. Although it was leveled by a bombing raid during the Battle of Monte Cassino of World War II, it has been painstakingly restored. A vacant, weed-filled lot in front of the church marks the place where my grandmother's house, which was not rebuilt after the war, once stood.

Up until 1993 there existed, in the Federal Hill section on the west side of Providence, Rhode Island, *Santo Eraclio, Vescova e Martire,* the Women's Society of Saint Eraclio. Amazingly, this society consisted solely of women who emigrated to Providence from Pietravairano and who had been members of the Parish of Saint Eraclio in Italy. Although first founded as a men's organization on 24 November 1901, a branch for women was established on 13 September 1949.

Saint Eraclio's intrigue is that he is the patron saint of the village of Pietravairano, but he has never been recognized by the Vatican. Here is Saint Eraclio's story, as related by Anna Caduto, in her words, to my sister, Linda Caduto, in the spring of 1986.

> Saint Eraclio was a young boy in Africa whose father was a great king. One day, the king called his son aside and told him that some day he would inherit the whole kingdom. The boy replied that he would rather be a Catholic priest. The father was very displeased by this.
>
> For the next several years, the boy grew into a young man and, as he grew, he helped people all over his country. When he became a young adult, he studied and was ordained as a priest. After much hard work, Father Eraclio attained the status of bishop.
>
> In the years that followed, a great war broke out in Africa. The king and Bishop Eraclio found themselves on opposing sides. The king murdered Bishop Eraclio, his son, placed his dismembered body in a coffin and floated it out to sea. After many months, the coffin floated up on the beach in Pietravairano, Italy. The townspeople opened the coffin and found, to their surprise, a very much alive Bishop Eraclio!
>
> After his rescue, the bishop traveled all over Italy, where he performed good deeds. He even visited Rome. After his death, because it was they who had found him, the people of Pietravairano made Saint Eraclio their patron saint.

After reading this story, you would be surprised to learn that Pietravairano is about 20 miles (32 kilometers) from the seashore! You may also wonder at the meaning of the violence in this tale. By looking deeper, it becomes clear that the events symbolize the fact that the son must completely remove himself from his father's ways in order to be true to himself, to honor his own beliefs. Ultimately, he must remake himself entirely and create a new life from the old. Parents, too, will find a message here. The story says it is important to support the growth of children when they are acting out of well-considered good intentions, even when they choose a path in life different than one's own. Saint Eraclio's saga shows how we may discover hidden layers of meaning wrapped within the simple tales that live in our midst.

—*Michael John Caduto*
Union Village, Vermont

SOURCES

Some of the information in the opening chapter, "Traditional Italian Tales and Storytelling," comes from several books that I used as references for background material on Italian tales, traditional Italian storytelling and fairy tales. These include *Italian American Folklore: Proverbs, Songs, Games, Folktales, Foodways, Superstitions, Folk Remedies, and More* by Frances M. Malpezzi and William M. Clements (Little Rock, Arkansas: August House Publishers, 1992); *Italian Folktales in America: The Verbal Art of an Immigrant Woman* by Elizabeth Mathias and Richard Raspa (Detroit: Wayne State University Press, 1985); *Italian Folktales* by Italo Calvino (New York: Pantheon, 1956, 1980); and *Beyond the Looking Glass: Extraordinary Works of Fairy Tale & Fantasy,* edited by Jonathan Cott (New York: Pocket Books, 1973). The information about traditional storytelling in the province of Veneto, Italy, is found in *Italian American Folklore.*

Two additional books that I recommend are *South Italian Folkways in Europe and America: A Handbook for Social Workers, Visiting Nurses, School Teachers, and Physicians* by Phyllis H. Williams (New York: Russell and Russell, 1969), and *The Two Rosetos* by Carla Bianco (Bloomington: Indiana University Press, 1974).

When raising children, there are some practical concerns that transcend time and place. The story "The Crimson Elf" is a wonderful, dark fantasy involving an evil ogre, a malevolent elf, a frightening run through a dark forest and a house in the woods made of sweets and cookies. Here, a healthy dose of fear encourages children to obey and stay close to their parents. The original version, from *Italian Folktales in America*, pp. 213–217, is called "The Bloodred Evil Elf."

The story "The Golden Stone" is also retold from a version found in *Italian Folktales in America*, pp. 169–174. In its original form as "The Stone of Gold," the story dwells more on the king's jealousy and possessiveness. In my retelling, however, this message becomes implicit. Instead, I have focused on the powers of Francesco's faith in true love over a marriage of convenience and on his strong belief in the equality of all people, his distrust of wealth and his close relationship with the natural world. The daughter, Leonora, plays an unusual role in that she helps her father in the fields. She has a mind of her own, and her parents respect her wishes.

"A Mountain of Contentment" appears in one of its original forms as the tale "The Three Brothers" in *Tales Merry and Wise* by Rose Laura Mincieli (New York: Henry Holt and Co., 1958), pp. 90–95. In this story from the Bari region by the Adriatic Sea, the purpose of the journey of the three brothers is that of getting bread for the family to eat. Here, I have brought out the deeper lessons of the story: faith, courage, contentment and obedience. As I sat with this tale, the element of fantasy grew increasingly stronger. This shows up in the old man's appearance, his home in a hollow tree and the nature of the woman who lives on the mountaintop.

Another version of this tale, "I Tre Orfani," is found in *Racconti Popolari Calabresi*, vol. I, story no. 41, edited by Raffaele Lombardi Satriani, (Naples, 1953). This version is adapted as "The Three Orphans" in *Italian Folktales* by Italo Calvino, pp. 482–484. These forms have their roots in Tiriolo, Calabria, in southern Italy.

"Frog Princess" is a pleasant reversal of romantic fortune when compared with the more common story of "The Frog Prince," which has appeared in many forms. There are more than three hundred versions of this story found in Europe. One Italian version, called simply "The Frog," is found in *The Violet Fairy Book*, edited by Andrew Lang (New York: Dover Publications, Inc., 1966), pp. 311–315. Another primary source from Italy is "La Moglie Trovata Colla Frombola" in *Novelline Popolari Italiane* by Domenico Comparetti (Turin: Ermanno Loescher, 1875), pp. 16–18. A recent picture-book adaptation is found in *The Frog Princess* by Laura Cecil (New York: Greenwillow Books, 1994). *Siberian and Other Folk Tales* by C. Fillingham Coxwell (London: The C.W. Daniel Co., 1925), pp. 712–720, has an interesting, lengthy variation told entirely in verse. A French form, "Petit Jean and the Frog," is found in *The Borzoi Book of*

French Folktales by Paul Delarue (New York: Knopf, 1956), pp. 109–118. Two Greek versions include "The Enchanted Lake" from *Folktales of Greece* by Georgios A. Megas (Chicago: University of Chicago Press, 1970), pp. 49–54, and "The Animal Wife" from *Modern Greek Folktales* by R.M. Dawkins (London: Oxford University Press, 1953), pp. 96–103.

I have transformed the story "The Land of Eternal Life" more than any other tale in this book. I expanded the true heart of this story, "Una Leggenda della Morte" (dialetto Veronese) by Arrigo Balladoro, which was found in a journal of Italian folklore, *Lares*, vol. 1, (Rome: Ermanno Loescher & Co., 1912), pp. 223–226, well beyond the lesson of the original. The raw, original version does not go beyond Gennaro's discovery of the truth that no one can live forever. It does, however, contain a tiny germ of the notion that it is possible to attain eternal life. I took this seed and nurtured it in my retelling.

I also discovered two other intriguing forms of this tale. A story from Turkey, "Youth Without Age and Life Without Death," is found in *Favorite Folktales from Around the World*, edited by Jane Yolen (New York: Pantheon Books, 1986), pp. 457–465. This version also appears in *Folk Tales of All Nations* by F.H. Lee (New York: Coward McCann, 1930), pp. 935–942. *The Crimson Fairy Book*, edited by Andrew Lang (New York: Dover Publications, Inc., 1967), pp. 178–191, contains a German variation of this tale, "The Prince Who Would Seek Immortality."

"Books of Wisdom" is the only story whose origin is a bit fuzzy. I first noticed it as "The Sibylline Books" in *Last Chance to See* by Douglas Adams and Mark Carwardine (New York: Ballantine, 1990), pp. 215–218. Although Adams does not mention it in the written text, in the audiocassette version of his book he identifies this story as coming from the Mediterranean. After my lengthy research to find another version of this tale proved fruitless, I decided to include the story here for several reasons. Primarily, I feel a strong, immediate connection to this story because the small city it describes could easily be one of hundreds that dot the Italian countryside. The wise, curmudgeonly old woman, with her strong will and wry sense of humor, reminds me of several of my elderly, female Italian relations. Finally, the story carries such a compelling message for our times that it begged to be included in this collection of Italian tales, which are also from the Mediterranean region.